The Velveteen Rabbit

By MARGERY WILLIAMS

Illustrated by

DAVID JORGENSEN

ALFRED A. KNOPF PUBLISHERS · NEW YORK

Designed by Antler & Baldwin Design Group

As adapted by Mark Sottnick for the video version of
THE VELVETEEN RABBIT
narrated by Meryl Streep

Library of Congress Cataloging in Publication Data
Bianco, Margery Williams, 1880–1944. The velveteen rabbit.
Summary: By the time the velveteen rabbit is dirty, worn out,
and about to be burned, he has almost given up hope
of ever finding the magic called Real.
1. Children's stories, American. [1. Toys—Fiction]
I. Jorgensen, David, ill. II. Title.
PZ8.9.B47Ve 1985 [Fic] 85-4257
ISBN 0-394-87711-X ISBN 0-394-87712-8 (book/cassette)

To my three sons,
David, Matthew, and Peter

– D.J.

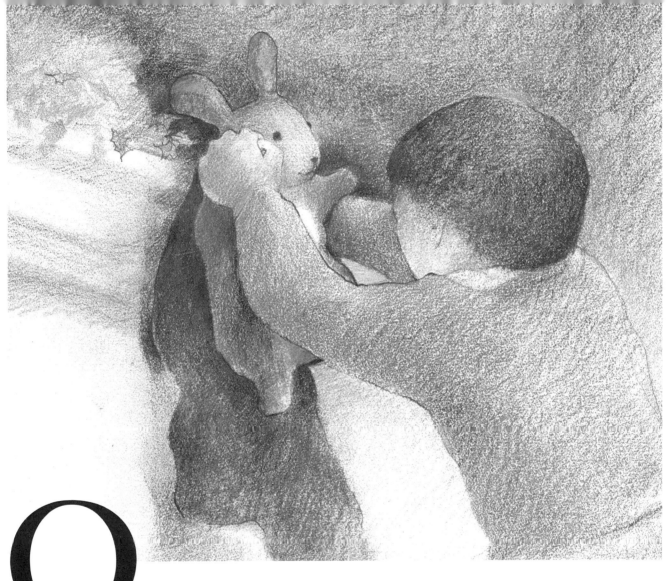

Once, there was a velveteen rabbit, and in the beginning he was really splendid. He was fat and bunchy, just as a rabbit should be; his coat was brown and white and was very soft. He had real thread whiskers, and his ears were lined with pink satin. On Christmas morning, when he sat wedged in the top of the Boy's stocking, with a sprig of holly between his paws, the effect was charming.

Of course there were other toys that Christmas, nuts and oranges and a toy engine, and chocolate almonds and a clockwork mouse, but the Rabbit was quite the best of all. For at least two hours the Boy loved him, and then Aunts and Uncles came to dinner, and there was a great rustling of tissue paper and unwrapping of parcels, and in the excitement of looking at all the new presents the Velveteen Rabbit was forgotten.

For a long time he lived in the toy cupboard or on the nursery floor, and no one thought very much about him. He was naturally shy, and being only made of velveteen, some of the more expensive toys made fun of him. The mechanical toys, like the model train, were very stuck-up and boasted that they were real.

But the Rabbit could not claim to be a model of anything, for he didn't know that real rabbits existed; he thought they were all stuffed with sawdust like himself, and he understood that sawdust was quite out-of-date. Even Timothy, the jointed wooden lion, who was made by disabled soldiers, and should have had broader views, put on airs. Between them all the poor little Rabbit was made to feel very insignificant and commonplace, and the only person who was kind to him at all was the Skin Horse.

The Skin Horse had lived longer in the nursery than any of the others. He was so old that his brown coat was bald in patches and showed the seams underneath, and most of the hairs in his tail had been pulled out to string bead necklaces. He was wise, for he had seen a long succession of mechanical toys arrive to boast and swagger, and by-and-by break their mainsprings and pass away. He knew that they were only toys, and would never turn into anything else. For nursery magic is very strange and wonderful, and only those playthings that are old and wise and experienced like the Skin Horse understand all about it.

"What is REAL?" asked the Rabbit one day. "Does it mean having things that buzz inside you and a stick-out handle?"

"Real isn't how you are made," said the Skin Horse. "It's a thing that happens to you. When a child loves you for a long, long time, not just to play with, but REALLY loves you, then you become Real."

"Does it hurt?"

"Sometimes." For he was always truthful. "When you are Real you don't mind being hurt."

"Does it happen all at once, like being wound up, or bit by bit?"

"It doesn't happen all at once. You become. It takes a long time. That's why it doesn't often happen to people who break easily, or who have sharp edges, or who have to be carefully kept. Generally, by the time you are Real, most of your hair has been loved off, and your eyes drop out and you get loose in the joints and very shabby.

"But these things don't matter at all, because once you are Real you can't be ugly, except to people who don't understand."

"I suppose *you* are Real?" And then he wished he had not said it, for he thought the Skin Horse might be sensitive. But the Skin Horse only smiled.

"The Boy's Uncle made me Real. That was a great many years ago; but once you are Real you can't become unreal again. It lasts for always."

The Rabbit sighed. He thought it would be a long time before this magic called Real happened to him. He longed to become Real, to know what it felt like; and yet the idea of growing shabby and losing his eyes and whiskers was rather sad. He wished that he could become it without these uncomfortable things happening to him.

There was a person called Nana who ruled the nursery. Sometimes she took no notice of the playthings lying about, and sometimes, for no reason whatever, she went swooping about like a great wind and hustled them away in cupboards. She called this "tidying up," and the playthings all hated it, especially the tin ones. The Rabbit didn't mind it so much, for wherever he was thrown he came down soft.

One evening, when the Boy was going to bed, he couldn't find
the china dog that always slept with him. Nana was in a hurry, and it
was too much trouble to hunt for china dogs and seeing that the toy
cupboard door stood open, she made a swoop.

"Here, take your old Bunny! He'll do to sleep with you!"

That night, and for many nights after, the Velveteen Rabbit slept
in the Boy's bed. At first he found it rather uncomfortable, for the
Boy hugged him very tight, and sometimes he rolled over on him,
and sometimes he pushed him so far under the pillow that the Rabbit
could scarcely breathe.

And he missed his talks with the Skin Horse during those long moonlight hours in the nursery, when all the house was silent.

But very soon he grew to like it, for the Boy used to talk to him, and made nice tunnels for him under the bedclothes, and they had splendid games together, in whispers. And when the Boy dropped off to sleep, the Rabbit would snuggle down close under his little warm chin and dream, with the Boy's hands clasped close around him all night long.

And so time went on, and the little Rabbit was very happy—so happy that he never noticed how his beautiful velveteen fur was getting shabbier and shabbier, and his tail was coming unsewn, and all the pink rubbed off his nose where the Boy had kissed him.

Spring came, and they had long days in the garden, for wherever the Boy went the Rabbit went too. He had rides in the wheelbarrow, and picnics on the grass, and lovely fairy huts built for him under the raspberry canes behind the flower border.

One time the Boy was called away suddenly, and the little Rabbit was left out on the lawn until long after dusk. Nana had to come and look for him with the candle because the Boy was so worried about the Rabbit he couldn't go to sleep unless the Rabbit was safely home. He was wet through with the dew and quite earthy from diving into the burrows the Boy had made for him in the flower bed.

Nana grumbled, "You must have your old Bunny! Fancy all that fuss for a toy!"

"Give me my Bunny! You mustn't say that. He isn't a toy. He's REAL!"

When the little Rabbit heard that, he was happy, for he knew what the Skin Horse had said was true at last. The nursery magic had happened to him, and he was a toy no longer. He was Real. The Boy himself had said it.

That night he was almost too happy to sleep, and so much love stirred in his little sawdust heart that it almost burst. And into his boot-button eyes, that had long ago lost their polish, there came a look of wisdom and beauty, so that even Nana noticed it next morning when she picked him up, and said, "I declare if that old Bunny hasn't got quite a knowing expression!"

That was a wonderful summer!

Near the house where they lived there was a wood, and in the long
June evenings the Boy liked to go there with the Velveteen Rabbit to
play. And each day, before the Boy wandered off to pick flowers, or play
at brigands among the trees, he made the Rabbit a little nest among the
bracken. He was a kind-hearted little Boy and he liked Bunny to be
comfortable. One evening, the Rabbit was sitting there alone, watching
the ants. Suddenly he saw two strange beings creep out of the tall
bracken near him.

They were rabbits like himself, but quite furry and brand-new.
They must have been very well made, for their seams didn't show at all,
and they changed shape in a queer way when they moved; one minute
they were long and thin and the next minute fat and bunchy, instead of
always staying the same like he did.

They stared at him, and the little Rabbit stared back. And all the
time their noses twitched.

"Why don't you get up and play with us?" one of them asked.

"I don't feel like it," said the Rabbit, for he didn't want to explain
that he had no clockwork.

"I don't believe you can!"

"I can! I can jump higher than anything!" He meant when the Boy threw him, but of course he didn't want to say so.

"Can you hop on your hind legs?"

That was a dreadful question, for the Velveteen Rabbit had no hind legs at all! He sat still in the bracken, and hoped the other rabbits wouldn't notice.

"I don't want to!" he said again.

But the wild rabbits have very sharp eyes. And this one stretched out his neck and looked.

"He hasn't got any hind legs!" And he began to laugh.

"I have! I have got hind legs! I am sitting on them!"

"Then stretch them out and show me, like this!" And he began to whirl around and dance.

"I don't like dancing. I'd rather sit still!"

But all the while he was longing to dance, for a funny new tickly feeling ran through him, and he felt he would give anything in the world to be able to jump about like these rabbits did.

The strange rabbit stopped dancing, and came quite close.

"He doesn't smell right! He isn't a rabbit at all! He isn't real!"

"I *am* Real! I am Real! The Boy said so!" And he nearly began to cry.

Just then there was a sound of footsteps, and the Boy ran past near them, and with a stamp of feet and a flash of white tails the two strange rabbits disappeared.

"Come back and play with me! Oh, do come back! I *know* I am Real!"

But there was no answer. The Velveteen Rabbit was all alone.

"Oh, dear! Why did they run away like that? Why couldn't they stay and talk to me?"

For a long time he sat very still, watching the bracken, and hoping that they would come back. But they never returned, and presently the sun sank lower and the little white moths fluttered out, and the Boy came and carried him home.

W eeks passed, and the little Rabbit grew very old and shabby, but the Boy loved him just as much. He loved him so hard that he loved all his whiskers off, and the pink lining to his ears turned grey. He even began to lose his shape, and he scarcely looked like a rabbit any more, except to the Boy. To him he was always beautiful, and that was all that the little Rabbit cared about. He didn't mind how he looked to other people, because the nursery magic had made him Real, and when you are Real, shabbiness doesn't matter.

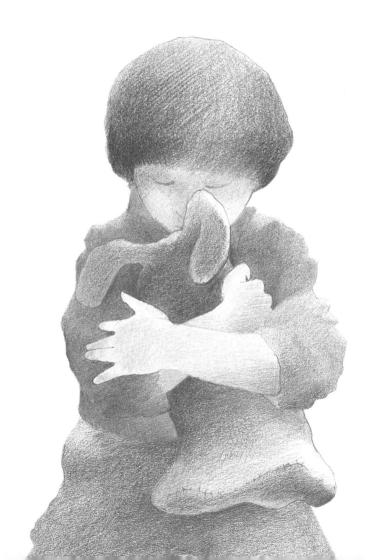

And then, one day, the Boy was ill.

His face grew very flushed, and he talked in his sleep, and his little body was so hot that it burned the little Rabbit when he held him close. Strange people came and went in the nursery, and a light burned all night, and through it all the little Velveteen Rabbit sat guard and never stirred.

It was a long weary time, for the Boy was too ill to play, but he knew that the Boy needed him.

And while the Boy lay half asleep, the little Rabbit crept up close to the pillow and whispered all sorts of delightful plans for when the Boy would be well again. They would go out in the garden among the flowers and butterflies and play splendid games in the raspberry thicket, just the way they used to.

At last the fever turned, and the Boy got better. He was able to sit up in bed and look at picture-books, while the little Rabbit cuddled close at his side.

And one day, they let him get up and dress.

They had carried the Boy out on to the balcony, wrapped in a shawl. The little Rabbit sat tangled up among the bedclothes, listening.

The Boy was going to the seaside tomorrow. Everything was arranged, and now it only remained to carry out the doctor's orders. The room was to be disinfected, and all the books and toys that the Boy had played with in the bed must be burnt.

"Hurray!" thought the little Rabbit. "To-morrow we shall go to the seashore!"

Just then Nana caught sight of him. "How about his old Bunny?"

"*That?*" said the doctor. "Why, it's a mass of scarlet fever germs!—Burn it at once. What? Nonsense! Get him a new one. He mustn't have that any more!"

And so the little Rabbit was put into a sack with the old picture-books and a lot of rubbish, and carried out to the end of the garden behind the fowl-house. That was a fine place to make a bonfire, only the gardener was too busy just then to attend to it. He had the potatoes to dig and the green peas to gather, but next morning he promised to come quite early and burn the whole lot.

That night the Boy slept in a different bedroom, and he had a new bunny to sleep with him. It was a splendid bunny, all white plush with real glass eyes, but the Boy was too excited to care very much about it. For to-morrow he was going to the seashore, and that in itself was such a wonderful thing that he could think of nothing else.

And while the Boy was asleep, the little Rabbit lay among the old picture-books in the corner behind the fowl-house, and he felt very lonely.

He was shivering a little, for he had always been used to sleeping in a nice warm bed, and by this time his coat had worn so thin and threadbare from hugging that it was no longer any protection to him. Nearby he could see the thicket of raspberry canes in whose shadow he had played with the Boy on bygone mornings.

He thought of those long sunlit hours in the garden—how happy they were—and a great sadness came over him. He seemed to see them all pass before him, each more beautiful than the other, the flower bed, the quiet evenings in the wood when he lay in the bracken and the little ants ran over his paws; the wonderful day when he first knew that he was Real.

And he thought of the Skin Horse, so wise and gentle, and all that he had told him. And a tear, a real tear, trickled down his little shabby velvet nose and fell to the ground.

And then a wonderful thing happened. For where the tear had fallen grew a mysterious flower, not at all like any other that grew in the garden. It was so beautiful that the little Rabbit forgot to cry, and just sat there watching it. Then suddenly the blossom opened, and out stepped the loveliest fairy in the whole world.

She came close to the little Rabbit and gathered him up in her arms and kissed him on his velveteen nose that was all damp from crying.

"Little Rabbit, don't you know who I am?"

The Rabbit looked up at her, and it seemed to him that he had seen her face before, but he couldn't think where.

"I am the nursery magic Fairy. I take care of all the playthings that the children have loved. When they are old and worn out and the children don't need them any more, then I come and take them away with me and turn them into Real."

"Wasn't I Real before?"

"You were Real to the Boy, because he loved you. Now you shall be Real to everyone."

And she held the little Rabbit close in her arms and flew with him into the wood.

It was light now, for the moon had risen. All the forest was beautiful, and the fronds of the bracken shone like frosted silver. In the open glade between the tree-trunks the wild rabbits danced with their shadows on the velvet grass, but when they saw the Fairy they all stopped dancing and stood round in a ring to stare at her.

"I've brought you a new playfellow. You must be very kind to him and teach him all he needs to know in Rabbitland, for he is going to live with you for ever and ever!"

And she kissed the little Rabbit again.

"Run and play, little Rabbit!"

But the little Rabbit sat quite still for a moment and never moved. For when he saw all the wild rabbits dancing around him he remembered about his hind legs. And he didn't want them to see that he was made all in one piece. He did not know that when the Fairy kissed him that last time she had changed him altogether.

And he might have sat there a long time, too shy to move, if just then something hadn't tickled his nose, and before he thought what he was doing he lifted his hind toe to scratch it.

He actually had hind legs! Instead of dingy velveteen he had brown
fur, soft and shiny, his ears twitched by themselves, and his whiskers
were so long that they brushed the grass.

He gave one leap and the joy of using those hind legs was so great
that he went springing about the turf on them, jumping sideways and
whirling around as the others did. He grew so excited that when at last
he did stop to thank the Fairy she had gone.

He was a Real Rabbit at last, at home with the other rabbits.

Autumn passed, and winter, and in the spring, while the Boy was out playing in the wood, two rabbits crept out and peeped at him. One of them was brown all over, but the other had markings under his fur, and about his little soft nose and his round black eyes there was something familiar, so that the Boy thought to himself:

"Why, he looks just like my old Bunny that was lost when I had scarlet fever!"

But he never knew that it really was his own Bunny, come back to look at the child who had first helped him to be Real.